• nursery collection •

ONCE UPON A TIME

4 well-loved nursery tales

Illustrated by Susie Lacome

TEMPLAR

THE THREE LITTLE PIGS

Once upon a time, three little pigs set out to seek their fortune. "Beware of the big, bad wolf," their mother warned them as they set off into the woods. Very soon, they met a man carrying a bundle of straw. "May I have some straw to build a house?" asked the first little pig. "Certainly," said the man, and the little pig set to work. The other two pigs walked on through the woods. Very soon, the two little pigs met a man carrying a bunch of sticks.

"May I have some sticks to build a house?" asked
the second little pig.
"Certainly," said the man, and the little pig set to work.
The third little pig wandered on alone until he met a
man pulling a cartload of bricks.
"May I have some bricks to build a house?" asked the pig.
"Certainly," said the man, and the little pig set to work.
The big, bad wolf was lurking in the woods when he
came across the house of straw.
Through the window, he saw the first little pig.

"Little pig, little pig, let me come in!"

"Not by the hairs on my chinny-chin-chin!" cried the pig.

"Then I'll huff, and I'll puff," said the big, bad wolf, "and I'll blow your house down!"

So he huffed and he puffed, and he blew the house down, and the first little pig ran squealing through the woods, to his brother's house of bricks.

Next, the wolf found the house of sticks. Through the window, he saw the second little pig. "Little pig, little pig, let me come in!"

"Not by the hairs on my chinny-chin-chin!"

"Then I'll huff, and I'll puff," said the big, bad wolf, "and I'll blow your house down!"

So he huffed, and he puffed, and he blew the house down!

The second little pig ran squealing to his brother's house of bricks.

When the wolf reached the house of bricks, he peered
through the window and saw all three little pigs together.
"Little pigs, little pigs, let me come in!"
"Not by the hairs on our chinny-chin-chins!" they cried.
The wolf huffed and puffed – but he couldn't blow the
house down, so he climbed up onto
the roof. The wolf was going to
climb down the chimney to
catch the three little pigs!
But the little pigs had
a plan too!

They pushed a cooking pot onto the fire, just as the wolf fell down the chimney – SPLASH! into the boiling water; and that was the end of the big, bad wolf!
The three little pigs lived happily ever after, safe in the house of bricks.

GOLDILOCKS AND THE THREE BEARS

Once upon a time, three bears lived in a little house in the woods. There was Father Bear, Mother Bear and Baby Bear.

Mother Bear had made porridge for breakfast. She poured it into a great big bowl, a middle-sized bowl and a tiny bowl. But the porridge was too hot, so the three bears went for a walk while it cooled off.

A little girl named Goldilocks was walking in the woods. When she found the three bears' house, she smelled the porridge, and crept inside.

First, she tried the porridge in the great big bowl – but it was too hot! Next, she tried the porridge in the middle-sized bowl – but it was too cold! Then, she tried the porridge in the tiny bowl. It was just right, so she ate it all up!

When she had finished, Goldilocks felt very full, so she decided to sit down. First, she sat in Father Bear's great big chair – but it was too high! Next, she sat in Mother Bear's middle-sized chair – but it was too wide!

Then, she sat in Baby Bear's tiny chair. It was just right! But Goldilocks was too heavy, and the chair broke! Goldilocks climbed the stairs to the bears' bedroom. First, she lay down in Father Bear's great big bed – but it was too hard! Next, she lay in Mother Bear's middle-sized bed – but it was too soft! Then, she lay down in Baby Bear's tiny bed. It was just right.
Goldilocks fell fast asleep, just as the bears returned and sat down for breakfast.

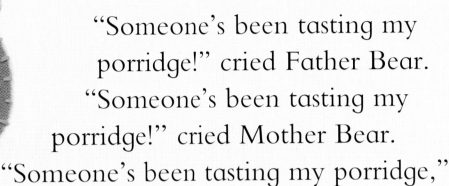

"Someone's been tasting my porridge!" cried Father Bear.
"Someone's been tasting my porridge!" cried Mother Bear.
"Someone's been tasting my porridge," cried Baby Bear, "and they've eaten it all up!"
Father Bear went to sit in his great big chair.
"Someone's been sitting in my chair!" cried Father Bear.
"Someone's been sitting in my chair!" cried Mother Bear.

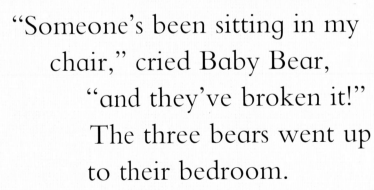

"Someone's been sitting in my chair," cried Baby Bear, "and they've broken it!"
The three bears went up to their bedroom.

"Someone's been sleeping in my bed!" cried Father Bear.
"Someone's been sleeping in my bed!" cried Mother Bear.
"Someone's been sleeping in my bed," cried Baby Bear,
"and she's still here!"
When Goldilocks woke and saw the three bears, she
was so startled that she jumped out of bed and ran all
the way home, never to come back!

LITTLE RED RIDING HOOD

Once upon a time, Little Red Riding Hood lived with her mother in a cottage in the woods. One day, Little Red Riding Hood's mother sent her to visit her poorly grandmother. She had not walked far when a wolf jumped out at her. Little Red Riding Hood was scared, but the wolf smiled and asked her where she was going. "To visit my grandmother," she replied.

"And where does your grandmother live, my dear?" asked the wolf, kindly. Too kindly!

"She lives in the house in the middle of the woods," said Little Red Riding Hood.

The wolf bounded away out of sight, and did not stop until he had reached the house in the middle of the woods! Once there, the wolf knocked on the door.

A voice inside called, "Who is it?"

"It is I, Grandmother. Little Red Riding Hood."

"Come in, my dear!" Grandmother called.

The wolf opened the door, leapt in, and roared at Little Red Riding Hood's grandmother! She was so scared that she leapt out of bed, and hid in a wardrobe!

A little while later, Little Red Riding Hood reached her grandmother's house, and knocked on the door.

A gruff voice inside called, "Who is it?"

"It is I, Grandmother. Little Red Riding Hood."

"Come in, my dear!" called the voice. Little Red Riding Hood opened the door, and stepped in. The wolf was sitting in bed, wearing Grandmother's bedclothes!

"What big ears you have, Grandmother!" Little Red Riding Hood exclaimed.

"All the better to hear you with," the wolf replied.

"What big eyes you have, Grandmother!" Little Red Riding Hood exclaimed.

"All the better to see you with," the wolf replied.

"And what big teeth you have, Grandmother!" Little Red Riding Hood cried.

"All the better to EAT you with!" the wolf sneered.

He was just about to swallow Little Red Riding Hood when...

a friendly woodcutter heard the commotion, and ran into the house! The wolf was so startled that he leaped out of Grandmother's bed, and ran away into the woods. He was never seen again!

"Help! Help!" cried a small voice from the wardrobe. The woodcutter opened the closet door, and out fell Red Riding Hood's grandmother, scared but safe!

The woodcutter helped Grandmother back into bed, then he walked Little Red Riding Hood through the woods to her mother's cottage, just in time for tea.

Puss-in-Boots

Once there lived an elderly miller with three sons. When the miller died, he left his beloved cat to his youngest son. The boy did not believe that the cat would be of any use to him, but the cat said, "Give me a sack and a pair of boots, and I shall bring you luck. You may call me Puss-in-Boots." Early the next day, Puss strode out of the mill house carrying a sack, and wearing a fine pair of boots.

Puss filled his sack with lettuce. When a rabbit saw the lettuce in the sack, it crept in, and Puss closed the sack tight! Off he ran to the King's castle to give him this special gift.

"Your Majesty, I come bearing a gift from my master," Puss-in-Boots declared.

"Who is your master?" the King asked Puss.

"He is the Marquis, your Majesty," Puss lied.

"Do thank him kindly for his gift!" said the King. Puss bowed and left the castle.

Early the next day, Puss strode out of the mill house, carrying his sack, and wearing a fine pair of boots. Puss filled his sack with corn. When two fat pheasants saw the corn, they crept in, and Puss closed the sack tight!

Off he ran to the King's castle to give him this special gift!
"Your Majesty, I come bearing a gift from my master,"
Puss declared.
"Well, do thank him kindly for his gift!" smiled the King.
Puss bowed and left the castle.
One day, Puss and the miller's son went down to the
river. Puss saw the King, riding in his carriage with his
daughter. He told his master to get into the water, while
he hid the boy's clothes behind a tree. The boy was
bathing in the river, when the King rode by.

"Help!" Puss cried out, "The Marquis is drowning, and somebody has stolen his clothes!"

The King jumped out of his carriage to save the boy.

"Now, come along with me," the King said. The boy climbed into the carriage beside the King's beautiful daughter, and they set off.

Puss ran ahead to a castle, belonging to an ogre.

"Tell the King that this castle belongs to the Marquis," ordered Puss-in-Boots, "or you shall be locked up!"
"No! I would rather turn myself into a dragon and burn down the castle," the ogre cried, "for I can turn myself into any creature, great or small!"
"Can you turn yourself into a lion?" asked Puss.
"Yes," said the ogre, and turned into a mighty lion.
"Into a mouse?" asked Puss.
"Yes," said the ogre, and turned into a tiny mouse. Puss leapt upon him and ate him whole!

Soon, the King arrived in his carriage, bringing his daughter, and the miller's son, with him. They made a handsome young couple, and the King was impressed by the charming boy. He was more impressed when Puss told him that the castle belonged to the Marquis!
The miller's son was glad that Puss had brought him good fortune, and asked the King's daughter to marry him!
They all lived happily ever after in the ogre's castle, and Puss, who never caught another creature, always wore his fine pair of boots.